Penguin  Readers

T0322190

Penguin Readers

MOOMIN SHORTS

ADAPTED FROM
TALES FROM MOOMINVALLEY

TOVE JANSSON

LEVEL

2

RETOLD BY ANNE COLLINS
ILLUSTRATED BY TOVE JANSSON
SERIES EDITOR: SORREL PITTS

PENGUIN BOOKS

UK | USA | Canada | Ireland | Australia
India | New Zealand | South Africa

Penguin Books is part of the Penguin Random House group of companies
whose addresses can be found at global.penguinrandomhouse.com.
www.penguin.co.uk www.puffin.co.uk www.ladybird.co.uk

Moomin Shorts adapted from *Tales from Moominvalley*
First published in Finland as *Det Osynliga Barnet*, 1962
Translation published in English by Ernest Benn Ltd, 1963
Published by Puffin Books, 1973
This Penguin Readers edition published by Penguin Books Ltd, 2024
001

Original text written by Tove Jansson
Text for Penguin Readers edition adapted by Anne Collins
Characters and artwork are the original creation of
Tove Jansson Copyright © Moomin Characters™, 2024
Design project management by Dynamo Ltd

The moral right of the original author and illustrator has been asserted

Printed and bound in Great Britain by Clays Ltd, Elcograf S.p.A.

The authorized representative in the EEA is Penguin Random House Ireland,
Morrison Chambers, 32 Nassau Street, Dublin D02 YH68

A CIP catalogue record for this book is available from the British Library

ISBN: 978-0-241-63674-9

All correspondence to:
Penguin Books
Penguin Random House Children's
One Embassy Gardens, 8 Viaduct Gardens,
London SW11 7BW

MIX
Paper | Supporting
responsible forestry
FSC
www.fsc.org   FSC® C018179

Penguin Random House is committed to a
sustainable future for our business, our readers
and our planet. This book is made from Forest
Stewardship Council® certified paper.

Contents

People in the stories

Moomintroll

Moominmamma
and Moominpappa

Snufkin

Little My

Snorkmaiden

A Hemulen

New words

candle

dragon

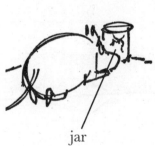

jar

paw

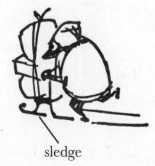

sledge

snout

Note about the stories

Tove Jansson (1914–2001) was from Finland. Her most famous stories are about the Moomin family. She wrote nine books about the Moomins and she drew beautiful pictures for her stories too. Today, people all **around*** the world love the Moomin family.

The Moomin family are Moominpappa, Moominmamma and Moomintroll. Sometimes, other people live with the Moomin family. In these stories, these people are Little My, Snorkmaiden and Snufkin.

Tove Jansson died in 2001 at the age of 86.

Before-reading questions

1 Look quickly at the stories and the pictures in the book. Are these sentences true or false?
  a There are four stories in the book.
  b The stories all happen in a city.
  c The first story is about a dragon.

2 Look online, and read about Tove Jansson.
  a What country was she from?
  b What other books did she write about the Moomins?

3 Look at the picture on page 40. What is happening, do you think?

*Definitions of words in **bold** can be found in the glossary on pages 61–62.

The Last Dragon in the World

One Thursday, Moomintroll caught a small dragon in the long grass in the garden. He was very **surprised**. He put it into a glass jar.

The dragon had six legs, a bright green head and yellow eyes. It **shone** in the sun and it looked wonderful. Moomin put the top on the jar. The dragon opened its mouth and it showed lots of small white teeth.

"This dragon is small, but it's very angry," thought Moomintroll.

He carried the jar home. "I'm going to keep you," he said quietly to the dragon. "I'll love you. You can sleep by my side at night. You'll start to like me. Then I'll take you swimming in the sea."

———

Moominpappa was in the garden but Moomintroll did not want him to see the dragon. He wanted to tell his friend Snufkin about it first.

Moomintroll **hid** the jar in his **paws** and he walked quietly to the back door of the house.

But, **suddenly**, Little My ran out. "What are you hiding in that jar?" she asked.

"I'm not hiding anything," said Moomintroll. He ran quickly up to his room and he put the jar on the table. The dragon showed its teeth again.

"Come out, little friend," said Moomintroll. He opened the top of the jar, then he closed the door. The dragon came out and it sat on the jar. Moomintroll put out his paw and he tried to **touch** the dragon. The dragon opened its mouth. It **blew** fire at Moomintroll and it **burned** him.

"Ow! You're angry!" Moomintroll said to the dragon. "Oh, my beautiful little baby!" He liked the dragon very much.

Moomintroll pulled out a small box from under his bed. There was cake, bread and an apple inside. He took out the food and he put it by the dragon. But the dragon did not want the food.

There was a big **fly** on the window. The dragon ran quickly to the window. It killed the fly and then it ate it. Then the dragon looked at Moomintroll.

"Well done!" Moomintroll said to the dragon. "I'm going to have my lunch now. Wait for me here and be good." He looked at the dragon with love in his eyes. "My little friend!" he said. Then he ran down and out to the **veranda**.

At lunch, Little My said, "Moomintroll is hiding something in a glass jar."

"Be quiet," said Moomintroll. "Mamma," he said to Moominmamma. "I would very much like to have my own small animal."

"What?" said Moominpappa. He looked up from his newspaper.

"Moomintroll has a new animal," said Moominmamma. "Does it **bite**?"

"It doesn't bite very hard," said Moomintroll.

"It's too small."

"Can we see it?" asked Little My. "Does it talk?"

Moomintroll was not happy. He wanted his dragon to be a **secret**. But you cannot have secrets in a family. They always know everything.

"I'm going down to the river after lunch," said Moomintroll. "Mamma, nobody must go into my room."

"Please don't go into Moomintroll's room, Little My," said Moominmamma.

Moomintroll finished his lunch. Then he walked through the garden and down to the river. He was happy about his dragon again.

———————

Moomintroll found Snufkin by the river. They sat together quietly for some minutes.

"Would you like to find a dragon?" asked Moomintroll.

"That's not possible," answered Snufkin. "There are no dragons in the world now."

"No, there is one," said Moomintroll. "It's in a glass jar. It has very small green paws."

Snufkin looked at Moomintroll. "That's not true," he said.

"Yes, it is true!" shouted Moomintroll. "I found a dragon!"

Snufkin was very surprised and Moomintroll was very happy.

Moomintroll and Snufkin went back to the house. They went quietly up to Moomintroll's room and opened the door. The jar was on the table, but the dragon was not there. Moomintroll looked everywhere – under the bed and behind the cupboard.

"Where are you, my little friend?" he asked.

"Moomintroll," said Snufkin. "It's up there on the **curtain**." Moomintroll looked. The dragon sat very high on the curtain.

"Oh no!" said Moomintroll. He pulled the bedclothes from his bed and he put them on the floor under the window. Then he took a **net** and he held it next to the dragon.

"Come down, little friend!" he said.

The dragon bit the net hard. Then it started flying **around** the room.

"Look!" shouted Moomintroll. "My dragon's flying!"

The dragon flew down and it bit Moomintroll's ear. "Ow!" he said. Then it flew to Snufkin and it sat on his **shoulder**. It closed its eyes and it made small, happy noises.

"My dragon likes you better than me," said Moomintroll sadly.

———

That afternoon, the Moomin family sat on the veranda. Snorkmaiden came home and everyone told her about the dragon. It sat on the veranda table by Snufkin's cup of coffee. Sometimes, it was angry, and then it burned the table.

"It's very nice," said Snorkmaiden. "What's its name?"

"It doesn't have a name," said Moomintroll. "It's not special. It's only a dragon." He moved his paw slowly across the table and he touched one of the dragon's legs. The dragon blew fire at him and it burned the table again.

"The dragon is small now," said Little My, "but one day it will **become** bigger. Then it can burn the house!" She took some cake. The dragon ran across the table and it bit her paw hard.

"Ow!" said Little My angrily. "Why did it bite me?" She started to hit the dragon.

"There was a fly on the cake," said Moomintroll. "My little dragon only wanted the fly."

"But it isn't your dragon," said Little My. "It's Snufkin's dragon because it likes only him."

Snufkin laughed. "No, it's not true," he said. "The dragon will remember Moomintroll, and it will fly back to him." But the dragon flew on to Snufkin's shoulder. He took it and he put it under a big bowl.

Then Snufkin opened the glass door and he went into the garden. He closed the door behind him.

Moomintroll moved the bowl and the dragon came out quickly. It flew to the window. It looked sadly at Snufkin. Then its colour changed to grey and it began to cry.

Moomintroll opened the veranda door and the dragon flew into the garden.

"Why did you do that?" asked Snorkmaiden. "Now you can't catch it again."

"Go and find Snufkin," said Moomintroll sadly. "You can find the dragon on his shoulder. The dragon likes Snufkin better than me."

————

Snufkin sat by the river. The dragon came and it sat on his shoulder. It was very, very happy to find Snufkin again.

"Go away!" said Snufkin. He tried to push the dragon away. "Go home!"

"This dragon wants to stay with me," he thought. "And maybe it can live for a hundred years." He looked sadly at the small dragon. "You're nice," he said, "but I can't keep you. Do you understand? Moomintroll is my best friend."

The little dragon went away and it caught some flies. Then it flew up to Snufkin's hat and it slept in it. Snufkin started catching fish. He caught five. Then a boat came down the river. A young Hemulen drove it.

"Where are you going?" asked Snufkin.

"I'm just going down the river," said the Hemulen.

"Would you like some fish?" asked Snufkin. He gave the five fish to the Hemulen.

"And what do *you* want from *me*?" asked the Hemulen.

Snufkin gave the Hemulen his hat with the sleeping dragon. "Now listen," he said. "Take this with you. Leave it in a nice place with a lot of flies."

"Is that a dragon?" asked the Hemulen. "Does it bite? How often does it eat?"

"Put some flies and a little water next to the hat," said Snufkin. "After two days, you can leave it."

———

Moomintroll came to see Snufkin after the sun went down.

"Hello," said Snufkin. "Please sit down."

"Did you catch any fish today?" asked Moomintroll.

"Yes, I caught five fish," answered Snufkin.

Then Moomintroll said, "Does it shine at night?"

"What are you talking about?" asked Snufkin.

"I'm talking about the dragon," said Moomintroll.

"I don't know," said Snufkin. "Go home and look."

"But it flew away," said Moomintroll. "Did it come to you?"

"No, it didn't," said Snufkin. "Maybe it saw a fly and it forgot about us. Dragons do that. They're not special."

Moomintroll was quiet. Then he sat down in the grass next to Snufkin.

"The dragon went away," Moomintroll said. "Maybe that's a good thing."

Then Snufkin said, "Do you want to catch some fish tomorrow?"

"Of course!" said Moomintroll happily.

The Invisible Child

One dark and rainy evening, the Moomin family sat around the big veranda table. There were newspapers on the table. On top of the newspapers were lots of **mushrooms**. The family worked quietly together. They cleaned the mushrooms and they cut them.

Suddenly, the veranda door opened and their friend Too-ticky came inside. Her coat was wet from the rain. She held the door and she shouted to someone in the garden, "Come here!"

"Who are you talking to?" asked Moomintroll.

"Her name is Ninny," answered Too-ticky. The family waited but nobody came.

"She's very **shy**," said Too-ticky.

"She'll get wet from the rain," said Moominmamma.

"It doesn't matter," said Too-ticky. "She's **invisible**." Too-ticky sat down by the table. The family stopped working and they waited.

"Sometimes, people become frightened," said Too-ticky. "Then they become invisible. Ninny lived with a woman, but the woman didn't like her. She wasn't kind to Ninny. She didn't shout, but she said bad things to her quietly. And she laughed at her. Then Ninny started to become invisible.

"The woman gave Ninny to me. I took her home, but now I want her to stay with you. You can help her. Then maybe she will stop being invisble."

Everyone looked at Too-ticky, but nobody said anything. They listened to the rain on the top of the veranda. Then Moominpappa said, "Does she talk?"

"No," answered Too-ticky. "But the woman gave her a small **bell**. We can't see Ninny, but we can see the bell."

Too-ticky stood up and she went to the door again. "Ninny!" she shouted. After some minutes, the family heard the noise of a small bell. Then they saw it. It moved to the veranda.

"This is your new family," said Too-ticky. "They're very good people."

"Give the child a chair," said Moominpappa. "Does she know anything about mushrooms?"

"I don't know," answered Too-ticky. "I have to go now. I have some things to do."

Too-ticky left and the family sat quietly. They watched the chair and the bell.

Suddenly, a mushroom moved up from the table. Invisible paws cleaned it. Then the paws cut the mushroom and they put it in a bowl. Another mushroom moved up from the table.

"That's **exciting**!" said Little My.

"How can people see Ninny again?" asked Moominmamma. "Let's take her to a doctor."

"No," said Moominpappa. "She's very shy. Maybe she *wants* to be invisible."

Moominmamma went up to a room at the top of the house. The small bell went behind her. There was a bed in the room. Moominmamma put an apple, a glass of juice and three sweets by the bed. Then she said, "Sleep well, Ninny. Stay in bed tomorrow as late as you want. Tea will be ready for you in the morning."

Moominmamma left the room. She went down to the kitchen and she found an old book. It was her grandmother's book. There were lots of **recipes** inside. Moominmamma found a recipe

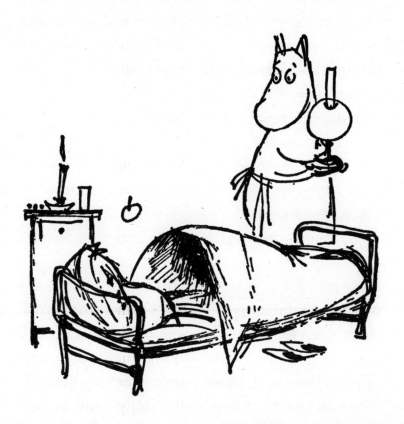

at the back of the book. She read it and then she smiled. "This recipe helps invisible people," she said. "Then other people can see them again. I'll make the recipe for Ninny."

The next morning, the small bell came slowly down from Ninny's room. Moomintroll waited for it. But the bell was not as exciting as Ninny's paws. They were very small but they were there. You could see her paws now, but you could not see Ninny.

Ninny went to the veranda and she got some tea. Moomintroll saw her cup. It moved to the table. Then Ninny ate some bread. Her cup and plate moved to the kitchen. Ninny washed them and she put them in a cupboard.

Moomintroll ran into the garden. Moominpappa and Moominmamma were there. Moominmamma sat high in an apple tree.

"Ninny has got paws! You can see them!" Moomintroll shouted.

"Good," thought Moominmamma. "Grandmother's recipe is working."

"That's great," said Moominpappa. "Maybe one day she can show her snout too. Talking to invisble people makes me sad. And they never answer me."

"Sssh!" said Moominmamma. Ninny's paws stood in the grass, in the middle of the apples.

"Hello, Ninny!" shouted Little My. "When are you going to show us your snout?"

"Be quiet, Little My," said Moomintroll. He ran to Ninny and he said, "Don't listen to Little My. You're safe here with us. Don't think about that bad woman. She can't take you away . . ."

Quickly, Ninny's paws started to become invisible again.

"Don't talk about that woman," said Moominmamma. "Don't say stupid things. Now come and get some apples." After some minutes, the family saw Ninny's paws again. They moved up a tree.

It was a beautiful autumn morning. The sun shone and everything was wet from the night's rain. The colours were strong and bright. Moominpappa brought some glass jars into the garden. The family started to cut the apples. They put the apples into the jars. Then Moominpappa carried the jars to the veranda. Little My sat in a tree and she sang the "Big Apple Song".

Suddenly, there was a loud noise. The family saw apples in the grass and there was lots of glass around the apples. They saw Ninny's paws too. But then her paws started to become invisible.

"Oh," said Moominmamma. "It doesn't matter about the jar. It was very old."

Ninny's paws came back again. Suddenly, Moomintroll shouted, "I can see her legs!"

Ninny's legs were very thin. Then the family saw a brown dress above the legs.

"Grandmother's recipe is very good," thought Moominmamma.

"That dress isn't a very nice colour," said Little My.

Ninny stayed with the family all day. In the evening, Moominmamma made a little pink dress for her. She made a ribbon for her hair too.

"But what colour is Ninny's hair?" thought Moominmamma. "Is it yellow or black?"

The next day, Ninny wore her new dress. Now you could see her body but not her face. She came down for her morning tea and she said, "Thank you all very much." Her voice was very high.

Little My laughed and she said, "You're talking! That's great. Do you know any good games?"

"No," said Ninny.

"That's OK," said Moomintroll happily. "We'll teach you some games."

After breakfast, Moomintroll, Little My and Ninny went to the river. They started to play. Ninny wanted to be kind, but she did not understand the games.

"Run, run!" shouted Little My.

Ninny ran, but then she stopped.

"What's the matter?" asked Little My.

"She can't play games," said Moomintroll quietly.

"She can't become angry," said Little My. "Listen," she said to Ninny. "You must learn to fight. Then maybe we can see your face."

"Yes, of course," said Ninny. But she was a little frightened.

Moomintroll and Little My stopped teaching Ninny games. They told her funny stories, but she did not like the stories. She never laughed at the right places.

For some days, Ninny's pink dress moved everywhere behind Moominmamma. Moominmamma stopped, and then the dress stopped too.

Moominmamma made her grandmother's recipe again. But now it did not work. Nobody could see Ninny's face.

————

One day, the family went to the beach. They wanted to pull their boat out of the sea for the winter. Ninny came too. But then she stopped and she started to cry.

"What's the matter with Ninny?" asked Moominpappa. "Is she frightened?"

Moominmamma spoke quietly to Ninny. Then she turned to the family and she said, "It's Ninny's first time by the sea. It's too big for her!"

"She's a very silly child," said Little My.

Moominmamma looked at her, then she said, "No, Little My. Ninny isn't silly." Then she said to the family, "Now let's pull the boat out of the sea. But it's very heavy. Let's ask Too-ticky to help us."

Too-ticky lived by the sea. The family went to her house.

"Hello," said Too-ticky. "How's the invisible child?"

"She's a little frightened today," said Moominmamma. "You can only see her snout. Can you help us with the boat?"

"Of course," said Too-ticky.

They pulled the boat out of the water.

Ninny stood on the beach and she looked at the sea. She did not move. Moominmamma looked down into the water. Then she said, "Nothing exciting happens to me. I want something exciting to happen."

Moominpappa came behind Moominmamma. He put out his paw and he touched Moominmamma's back.

He only wanted to play. He did not want to push Moominmamma into the water. But Ninny did not understand that and she wanted to help Moominmamma. Suddenly, the family saw Ninny's pink dress. It moved quickly across the beach. Ninny bit Moominpappa's leg with her small, invisible teeth.

"Ow!" shouted Moominpappa and his hat went into the water.

Suddenly, everybody saw Ninny. She stood on the beach. Her face was red and angry. "Don't push Moominmamma into the sea!" she shouted.

"I see her, I see her!" shouted Moomintroll. "She's very nice."

"No, she isn't," said Moominpappa. He looked at his leg. Then he sat down and he tried to take his hat out of the sea. But, suddenly, he went into the water.

"Oh," Ninny shouted, "that's very funny!" She laughed.

"She never laughed before," said Too-ticky. "She's a different child now. How did you change her? She's as bad as Little My."

"*We* didn't change her," said Moominmamma.

"My grandmother changed her." She started laughing too.

The Fir Tree

A Hemulen stood on top of the Moominhouse. There was a lot of snow and his yellow **mittens** were wet and cold. The Hemulen put his mittens on the roof. Then he found a **hatch** and he pushed it.

"The Moomin family are sleeping down there," said the Hemulen. "They're sleeping and they're sleeping and they're sleeping. But other people have to work hard because Christmas is coming."

Suddenly, the hatch opened and the Hemulen went down into the house. A lot of snow went with him.

"Oh no!" said the Hemulen. "Where are my yellow mittens?" He walked into the living room. He could not see his mittens, but he saw the Moomin family. Every winter, the family slept in the living room and they woke up in the spring.

"I was right. The family are sleeping. Christmas

is coming and I'm very tired!" the Hemulen shouted angrily.

Moomintroll started to wake up. "Is it spring now?" he asked.

"What do you mean?" said the Hemulen. "I'm not talking about spring. I'm talking about Christmas!" He left the room and he went up to the top of the house. He went out of the house again through the hatch.

"Mamma, wake up!" said Moomintroll to Moominmamma. "Something is happening. It's called Christmas." He touched Snorkmaiden on the shoulder and he said quietly, "Don't be frightened, but something bad is happening."

The Moomin family woke up. They went up to the hatch at the top of the Moominhouse. Then they went out through the hatch. They saw trees with snow and the river. The sky was blue but the weather was cold. It was colder than in April.

Moominpappa held some snow in his paw.

"What's this?" he asked. "Is this Christmas? Did it come from the ground or the sky?"

"It's snow, Pappa," said Moomintroll.

"It isn't very nice," said Moominpappa.

The Hemulen's **aunt** drove past the house on a sledge. There was a tree on the sledge. She saw the Moomin family and she was very surprised. She said, "You woke up! Then you must get a tree."

"But why?" asked Moominpappa.

"I have to go now," said the Hemulen's aunt. "I have some things to do. Find a tree before night."

"I don't understand," thought Moomintroll. "Do bad things happen at night?"

"Find a tree," said Moominmamma. "I'll make a fire."

———

Moominpappa and Moomintroll went to their friend Gaffsie's house. There was a big tree in her garden. Moominpappa and Moomintroll cut down the tree and they carried it to the river. Suddenly, Gaffsie ran to them. She carried paper bags in her arms. Her face was red and tired.

"What must we do with this tree?" asked Moominpappa.

Gaffsie did not answer the question but she said, "Christmas is coming and I have a lot of things to do."

Moominmamma was at home. She cleaned the snow from the veranda. A little woody sat on the veranda. It drank a cup of tea.

"We have got a tree," said Moomintroll. "But what do we do with it?"

"You must put beautiful things on it," said the woody quietly. Then it went away through the snow.

"Why must we put beautiful things on the tree?" asked Moominpappa. "It's difficult to hide in a beautiful tree. But maybe a beautiful tree will make Christmas happy!" Moominpappa and Moomintroll carried the tree into the garden. They put it down on the snow. Then the family found some beautiful things and they put them on the tree. They put a pretty red flower at the top.

The Hemulen's aunt came past the garden on her sledge. She drove it very quickly.

"Look at our Christmas tree!" shouted Moomintroll.

"Oh," said the Hemulen's aunt. "Your tree looks very strange. I must go now. I must get some food for Christmas."

"What do you mean?" asked Moomintroll. "What does Christmas eat?"

The Hemulen's aunt did not listen. "You have to make dinner for Christmas," she said. Then she went away.

Moominmamma worked hard all afternoon. She cooked lots of food for Christmas. She made cakes and biscuits and other things too. The Moomin family liked all these things.

"Is Christmas hungry?" asked Moominmamma.

"I don't know," said Moominpappa. He sat in the snow in his coat.

Night came. There were candles in the window of every house and under the trees too.

"Get some candles for Christmas," said Moominpappa.

Moomintroll went into the house and he found some candles. He put them in the snow around the tree. The candles burned brightly in the dark night. They were beautiful.

Then the Hemulen came. "Hello," said Moomintroll. "Is Christmas coming?"

The Hemulen sat down by one of the candles. He had some paper in his hand with people's names. He read the names. "Mother, Father, Gaffsie . . ." he said.

"Why are you reading these people's names?" asked Snorkmaiden.

"I have to find Christmas **presents** for them," said the Hemulen. He started to leave.

"Wait!" shouted Moomintroll. "What do you mean? And where are your mittens?"

The Hemulen went away and the Moomin family went into their house. "We must find presents for Christmas too," said Moomintroll.

Moominpappa found a pretty box. He wrote "For Christmas" on it. Snorkmaiden found a beautiful bowl. Moominmamma found a book with wonderful pictures. The family put the presents in the snow by the tree. Then they sat down and they waited for Christmas. But Christmas did not come.

Then the small woody came with lots of its friends.

"Happy Christmas!" said the woody shyly to the Moomin family. "Can we look? Your tree is wonderful."

"All the food is wonderful too," said another woody. "And the presents are beautiful!"

The candles burned brightly in the dark night. The woody and his friends sat quietly. They all looked at the tree.

Moominmamma said quietly to Moominpappa, "Can we give everything to the woody and his friends?"

"Yes, of course," said Moominpappa. "But will Christmas be angry?"

"It doesn't matter," said Moomintroll. "We can go inside the house and we can close the doors. We'll be safe there." He turned to the woody and he said, "You can have the tree and all the food and presents."

The woody was very happy and surprised. It stood next to the tree.

"We have to go now," said Moominpappa. The family went back to the veranda. They closed the door and they hid under the table.

Nothing happened.

Then the family looked out of the window. All the small animals sat around the fire. They ate and they drank and they opened presents. They put candles on the tree. They were very happy.

"Everything is fine," said Moominmamma. "But I'm very tired."

"I'm not frightened of Christmas now," said Moomintroll. "But maybe the Hemulen and Gaffsie didn't understand Christmas."

They found the Hemulen's yellow mittens and they put them by the veranda. Then the family went back to the living room. They slept, and they waited for spring.

During-reading questions

THE LAST DRAGON IN THE WORLD

1 What does Moomintroll find in the garden?
2 How does he carry it to the house?
3 Who does Moomintroll want to tell first about the dragon?
4 What does the dragon like to eat?
5 Why is Moomintroll sad about the dragon and Snufkin?
6 Why is Little My angry with the dragon?
7 "You're nice, but I can't keep you." Why does Snufkin say this?
8 What does Snufkin tell the Hemulen to do?

THE INVISIBLE CHILD

1 Who does Too-ticky visit one evening?
2 How is Ninny different from other children?
3 Why does she wear a small bell?
4 Where does Ninny sleep?
5 How does the recipe help invisible people?
6 Why do the Moomin family go to the beach?
7 What does Ninny think about the sea?
8 Why does she bite Moominpappa?

THE FIR TREE

1 Where are the Moomin family sleeping?
2 Why does Moomintroll wake up?
3 Where do Moominpappa and Moomintroll get a tree from?
4 What does the woody tell the Moomins to put on the tree?
5 What are the Moomin family's presents for Christmas?
6 What do the family give to the woody and his friends?
7 Why do the family hide under the table?
8 What happens to the Hemulen's yellow mittens?

After-reading questions

1 Which of the three stories do you like best? Why?

2 "You cannot have secrets in a family." Is this true, do you think?

3 Is Snufkin a good friend to Moomintroll, do you think?
Why/Why not?

4 How do these people help Ninny? Who does Ninny like best,
do you think?
a Too-ticky
b Moominmamma
c Moominpappa
d Moomintroll

5 "I'm not frightened of Christmas now," says Moomintroll.
What does he learn about Christmas?

6 Would you like to live with the Moomin family?
Why/Why not?

7 Would you like to read more stories about this family?
Why/Why not?

Exercises

1 **Are these sentences *true* or *false*? Write the correct answers in your notebook.**

1 The dragon has four legs. *false* *The dragon has six legs.*
2 Moomintroll and Snufkin are friends.
3 The dragon's favourite foods are cake, apples and bread.
4 The dragon does not bite.
5 The dragon can fly.
6 The dragon likes Moomintroll better than Snufkin.
7 The Hemulen gives Snufkin five fish.
8 The Hemulen takes the hat and the dragon.

2 **Choose the correct verb forms to complete these sentences in your notebook.**

1 Moomintroll **find** / *found* a small dragon in the garden.
2 The dragon **blew** / **blow** fire from its mouth.
3 "Moomintroll **is hiding** / **hide** something in a glass jar," said Little My.
4 "It doesn't **has** / **have** a name," said Moomintroll.
5 The dragon **flew** / **fly** into the garden.
6 Then it **sat** / **sitting** on Snufkin's shoulder.
7 "**Will** / **Would** you like some fish?" asked Snufkin.
8 That evening, Moomintroll **come** / **came** to see Snufkin.

3 Complete these sentences in your notebook, using the words from the box.

| invisible | becomes | bell | shy |
| mushrooms | Suddenly | recipe | ribbon |

1 People cannot see Ninny because she is ...*invisible*...

2 One evening, the Moomin family clean and cut ....

3 The family can hear Ninny's small ....

4 Ninny does not speak much because she is very ....

5 Moominmamma finds a .... from her grandmother.

6 She makes a .... for Ninny's hair.

7 Ninny .... frightened because the sea is very big.

8 ...., Moominpappa goes into the water.

4 Put these sentences in the correct order in your notebook.

a .... Moominmamma finds her grandmother's recipe book.

b .... Moominpappa goes into the water.

c .... Ninny breaks a glass jar in the garden.

d ...*1*... A woman gives Too-ticky an invisible child.

e .... The family pull their boat out of the sea.

f .... Suddenly, everybody can see Ninny.

g .... Too-ticky takes Ninny to the Moomin family.

h .... Ninny bites Moominpappa's leg.

5 **Complete the sentences in your notebook with the past simple form of the verb.**

1 The Moomin family _slept_ (**sleep**) every winter.

2 The Hemulen's aunt .... (**drive**) past the house.

3 Gaffsie .... (**not answer**) Moomintroll's question.

4 The little woody .... (**drink**) a cup of tea.

5 Moominpappa .... (**sit**) in the snow.

6 The family .... (**find**) presents for Christmas.

7 They waited for Christmas but it .... (**not come**).

8 The Moomins .... (**hide**) under the table.

6 **Write the correct answers in your notebook.**

1 Every winter, the Moomin family sleep in the _living room_.
   a kitchen   **b** living room   **c** bedroom

2 The Hemulen looks for his yellow ....
   a shoes   **b** hat   **c** mittens

3 Moomintroll puts .... around the tree.
   a candles   **b** cakes   **c** flowers

4 Snorkmaiden finds a beautiful ....
   a picture   **b** bowl   **c** book

5 The family hides under the ....
   a table   **b** bed   **c** veranda

6 They sleep and they wait for ....
   a Christmas   **b** spring   **c** summer

7 Who said this? Who did they say it to? Write the answers in your notebook.

Moomintroll

Moominmamma

Moominpappa

	Who said this?	Who to?
1 "My dragon likes you better than me."	*Moomintroll*	*Snufkin*
2 "Does it bite?"		
3 "Does she talk?"		
4 "It's Ninny's first time by the sea."		
5 "Did it come from the ground or the sky?"		
6 "What does Christmas eat?"		

8 Write the correct word in your notebook.

1	lefsi	*flies*	The dragon's favourite food.
2	nrub	....	Fire does this.
3	hudselor	....	A part of your body, near your head.
4	souhomrsm	....	The Moomin family clean and cut these.
5	elbl	....	Ninny wears this.
6	natu	....	Your father's or mother's sister.
7	eesdlg	....	You can ride on this in the snow.
8	rsstpeen	....	People give these to their families and friends at Christmas.

Project work

1 What happens to the dragon after the story ends, do you think? And what happens to Ninny? Write about them.

2 Some animals sleep in the winter. Look online, and find out about one of them. Tell a friend about the animal, or write about it.

3 Look online, and find out about Finland. Make a poster about it.

4 Work with some friends. Write and act one of these parts of a story:

   a The Moomin family are having tea on the veranda. The dragon bites Little My. (pages 16–17)

   b Ninny bites Moominpappa's leg. Moominpappa goes into the water. (pages 39–40)

   c The Moomin family give their tree and presents to the woody and his friends. (pages 50–51)

An answer key for all questions and exercises can be found at **www.penguinreaders.co.uk**

Glossary

around (prep.)
on every side of a person or thing

aunt (n.)
the sister of your mother or father

become (v.)
to start to be

bell (n.)
You move a *bell* and it rings
(= makes a high noise).

bite (v.)
An animal can *bite* you with its teeth.

blow (v.)
past tense: **blew**
A person or animal *blows* and air
comes out of their mouth.

burn (v.)
Fire *burns* people and then they
are not well or they die.

curtain (n.)
You put *curtains* in front of windows.
You close them and then it is dark.

exciting (adj.)
Something is *exciting*. You are very
happy about it.

fly (n.)
a very small animal with six legs.
It flies.

hatch (n.)
a small door

hide (v.)
past tense: **hid**
1) You *hide* something because you
do not want people to find it or
see it.
2) You *hide* in a place because you
do not want people to see you.

invisible (adj.)
No one can see an *invisible* person
or thing.

mittens (n.)
You wear *mittens* on your hands.
They are warm.

mushroom (n.)
it grows from the ground. It is small
and can be brown or white with a
round top. You can cook and eat
some *mushrooms*.

net (n.)
You use a *net* to catch fish or *flies*.

present (n.)
Some people give *presents* to other
people at Christmas or for their
birthdays.

recipe (n.)
A *recipe* tells you how to make a cake
or a dinner.

secret (n.)
Not many people know about
a *secret*.

shine (v.)
past tense: **shone**
to give or make light

shoulder (n.)
Your arm meets your body at
your *shoulder*.

shy (adj.)
A *shy* person does not like talking to
new people.

suddenly (adv.)
Something happens quickly and you
are *surprised*. It happens *suddenly*.

surprised (adj.)
Something happens and you did not
know about it. You are *surprised*.

touch (v.)
to put your fingers on something

veranda (n.)
a place outside a house. You can put
a table and chairs on it and you can
sit there.

Penguin 🐧 Readers

Visit **www.penguinreaders.co.uk**
for FREE Penguin Readers resources
and digital and audio versions of this book.